STAR WARS™

A GALAXY AT WAR

Penguin
Random
House

Editorial Assistant Lauren Nesworthy
Senior Designer David McDonald
Pre-Production Producer Kavita Varma
Producer Zara Markland
Managing Editor Sadie Smith
Design Manager Ron Stobbart
Creative Manager Sarah Harland
Art Director Lisa Lanzarini
Publisher Julie Ferris
Publishing Director Simon Beecroft

Lucasfilm Ltd.
Executive Editor Jonathan W. Rinzler
Art Director Troy Alders
Story Group Rayne Roberts, Pablo Hidalgo, Leland Chee

This edition published in 2016
First American Edition, 2015
Published in the United States by DK Publishing
345 Hudson Street, New York, New York 10014
DK, a Division of Penguin Random House LLC

First published as three separate titles: *Star Wars: Beware the Dark Side* (2007),
Star Wars: Epic Battles (2008), and *Star Wars: Ultimate Duels* (2011)

003–271024–May/14

A catalog record for this book is available
from the Library of Congress.

ISBN 978-1-4351-5415-5

Printed and bound in China

www.starwars.com
www.dk.com

A WORLD OF IDEAS:
SEE ALL THERE IS TO KNOW

STAR WARS™

A GALAXY AT WAR

DK

Contents

STAR WARS™

EPIC BATTLES

Written by Simon Beecroft

Jedi Knights
The Jedi use a
mysterious
energy called
the Force.
Jedi Knights
carry glowing
lightsabers
to defend
themselves.

What side are you on?

A long time ago, in a galaxy far, far away, a great and peaceful Republic existed. Each planet, large or small, made its voice heard in a huge Senate building on the capital planet, Coruscant. The Jedi Knights defended peace and justice everywhere. They ensured that arguments between planets were sorted out without violence or war.

Battle droids
The Trade
Federation built
many millions
of machine-
soldiers called
battle droids.
Each battle
droid carries a
deadly blaster
weapon.

Sadly, this peace was about to be smashed. A greedy business organization called the Trade Federation created an army and began to invade planets, starting with a small world called Naboo. As the conflict grew, the Republic later deployed its own army. With the galaxy at war, both sides learned too late that they had been manipulated by a deadly Sith Lord!

Sith Lord
The Sith have deadly evil powers. The Sith Lord Darth Sidious plots to destroy the Jedi and rule the entire galaxy.

Warmongers
The Trade Federation and other greedy business corporations take orders from the Sith and use their droid armies to attack the Republic.

Dark forces
The evil Sith
Lord Darth
Sidious, also
known as
Emperor
Palpatine, peers
from his black
cape. He is
flanked by his
trusted servant,
Darth Vader,
his red-caped
guards, and
battalions of
white-armored
stormtroopers.

The Sith were the greediest beings in the galaxy. The leader was called Darth Sidious and he was secretly controlling the Trade Federation. He wanted it to start a war that would put him in power as Emperor. He fooled everyone by pretending to be a kindly politician called Senator Palpatine. Palpatine became leader of the Senate, took control of the Republic's army, and forced every planet to obey him.

Hired hands
Sith Lords often hire assassins, spies, and bounty hunters to do their dirty work for them. Bounty hunters are skilled hunters who kidnap people for a fee.

A few brave people refused to accept Palpatine's evil Empire. They were called the Rebel Alliance—and they set out to free the galaxy.

This is the story of the Emperor's rise to power and his downfall at the hands of the brave-hearted Rebels. It is a story of great struggles on land and in space. From all-out attacks to deadly duels and fights with savage beasts, these battles are epic!

Rebels at the ready
Luke Skywalker, his twin sister Princess Leia, Han Solo, and the Wookiee Chewbacca all fight for the Rebel Alliance.

Legendary land battles

The galaxy first erupted into violence when the Trade Federation invaded Naboo. This peaceful planet was home to the Naboo people and a water-dwelling species called the Gungans. Two Jedi were sent to investigate: Qui-Gon Jinn and Obi-Wan Kenobi. With help from the Gungans, the Jedi rescued the Naboo Queen, Padmé Amidala.

Vile leaders
The Trade Federation's cowardly leaders land on Naboo only after their battle droids have captured the royal palace.

The Jedi took Queen Amidala to Coruscant to ask the Senate for its help. But the Senate was all talk and no action. Amidala would have to free her planet herself!

She and the Jedi returned to Naboo and battled their way to the hangar where their spaceships were housed. Then Amidala led an attack on the royal palace, fighting many battle droids. Elsewhere, the Gungans fought a battle-droid army. Now the Naboo pilots had to destroy the Trade Federation ship that was controlling the battle droids.

Swift strike
Qui-Gon slices a deadly battle droid in two as he helps Queen Amidala escape from her planet.

Back-up droid
Droideka are even more deadly than battle droids. They carry twin blaster weapons.

Return to Naboo
Qui-Gon Jinn and Obi-Wan Kenobi lead the attempt to recapture Queen Amidala's palace.

11

Gungan soldiers face the might of the Trade Federation's droid army.

Boss Nass
Queen Amidala asks the Gungan ruler, Boss Nass, to help her fight the invaders.

The deadly land battle between the Gungan army and the massed ranks of battle droids took place on a wide-open grassy plain. At first the Gungans were very clever. They activated special machines carried by their giant swamp lizards. These machines generated an energy bubble that protected the Gungan army from high-speed airborne missiles.

But the Gungans did not realize that battle droids could walk right through their shield. Now the two armies battled each other inside the shield. The Gungans fought bravely but could not hope to win against an endless supply of battle droids. It would take a space battle above Naboo to shut down the droid army.

Binoculars

Atlatl

Electropole

War weapons
Gungans use a variety of unusual weapons that fire balls of explosive energy called plasma. They hurl these balls into the air with catapults and throwing sticks called atlatls.

Energy shields
Gungan soldiers carry glowing energy shields into battle to protect themselves from blaster bolts fired by battle droids.

13

New leader
The Neimoidian leaders are joined by a powerful new ally, the former Jedi, Count Dooku.

Wheel droids
Sinister hailfire droids roll into battle on giant hoop wheels, while Republic gunships prepare to strike from above.

After the Republic learned that its enemies were creating huge droid armies, it was tricked into using a ready-made army to defend itself. Its Army consisted of millions of clone troopers—each clone was an identical copy of a single ultimate soldier. This hastily assembled army first saw action on a planet called Geonosis.

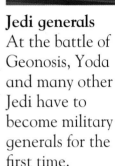

Jedi generals
At the battle of Geonosis, Yoda and many other Jedi have to become military generals for the first time.

Advance guard
Clone troopers blast their way toward the enemy, using special sight systems in their helmets to see through the dense smoke on the battlefield.

The droid armies attacked the Jedi in a large arena on Geonosis. When clone troopers joined the fray, led by Jedi Master Yoda, the battle spread outside the arena. Many Jedi and clone troopers were killed, but finally the droids and their masters retreated. This was the first battle of the famous Clone Wars.

Tarfful
One of the Wookiee leaders is called Tarfful. When the Republic's clone troopers, wheeled tanks, and walking guns go into battle against the droids, Tarfful and the Wookiees are right alongside them.

Droid armies attacked everywhere. One of the biggest battles took place on Kashyyyk. This planet was home to tall, furry creatures called Wookiees. The Wookiees and the Republic army fought on land and sea. But just as victory was in sight, it all went wrong. The Republic did not know that their clone troopers had been brainwashed to switch sides when they received a special signal.

When the clones received the signal, Order 66, they turned their weapons on their Jedi generals. The clones took orders only from the Sith. When Darth Sidious became Emperor, the clone troopers became his personal army, known now as stormtroopers. The Empire was born.

Assassination
When the Sith signal is received, every clone commander turns on the Jedi. Nearly all the Jedi leaders are killed. Aayla Secura is assassinated while fighting on the fungi planet, Felucia.

Walking tanks
The Empire's terrifying walking tanks, called AT-ATs, advance across the snow toward the Rebel base.

Great land battles took place in the time of the Empire, too. Many brave individuals joined the Rebel Alliance and fought against the Empire, though they had few weapons, vehicles, or other resources. The Emperor and Darth Vader put much of the Empire's military might toward crushing the Rebel Alliance.

Front line
The Rebels try to hold off the advancing AT-ATs with their heavy guns.

18

Rebel hangar
The Rebel base is a converted ice cave, with a massive hangar for vehicles.

Darth Vader discovered that the Rebels had built a secret base on the ice planet Hoth. His troops attacked it with great force. He sent in giant walking tanks called AT-ATs. The Rebels tried to hold off the AT-ATs for as long as they could, and even managed to destroy two of them. But eventually they were forced to flee and find another hiding place.

Enter Vader
Sith Lord Darth Vader enters the Rebel base, which is now a smoking ruin. He is flanked by stormtroopers equipped for missions in sub-zero conditions.

Scout trooper
Imperial scout troopers on flying speeder bikes chase down the Rebels when they land on Endor.

After the defeat at Hoth, the Rebels hid all over the galaxy. Palpatine hatched a plan to draw them out. He had once built a huge super-weapon called the Death Star, which the Rebels had destroyed. Now he built a second Death Star, knowing the Rebels would try to stop him. Then he would blow the Rebel fleet out of the sky.

Battle in the forest
Stormtroopers, backed up by a walking AT-ST cannon, do battle with Han and Chewbacca.

The Death Star was protected by a shield generator on the forest moon of Endor. A team of Rebels led by Luke Skywalker, Princess Leia, Han Solo, and Chewbacca went to Endor to destroy the generator. The Rebels faced a large Imperial army, but they were helped by natives called Ewoks. Together they suceeded in destroying the shield generator, and then the Rebel fleet was able to attack the Death Star.

Ewok attack
Small, determined Ewoks hurl rocks at stormtroopers in their well-planned attacks.

Rebel team
Han tries to break into the generator bunker while Leia holds off advancing stormtroopers.

Space battles

Many of the biggest battles in the galaxy took place in space. When the Trade Federation invaded Naboo, its massive battleships surrounded the planet. While the conflict raged on the ground, a handful of Naboo ships managed to take off and fly toward the battleships.

Feared fleet
Deadly Trade Federation vulture droid ships emerge from the ring-shaped Droid Control Ship.

Rookie pilot
Anakin is whisked into the space battle when the autopilot engages in the starfighter he is hiding in.

One of the Naboo ships was flown—at first, accidentally— by a nine-year-old boy called Anakin Skywalker. Anakin had Jedi abilities and was a superb pilot, although he had never flown a starship before. He managed to enter the Trade Federation's Droid Control Ship and fire torpedoes into its reactor room, escaping in his starfighter as the ship exploded. Anakin's incredible feat saved Naboo.

Brave strike
Starfighters avoid deadly laser blasts.

Blown away
The Control Ship sends instructions to every battle droid. When it is destroyed, the droids stop fighting.

Close combat
A Naboo starfighter narrowly avoids a direct hit as the Droid Control Ship fires at oncoming Naboo ships.

Jedi team
Anakin and Obi-Wan fly side-by-side in their fast Interceptors.

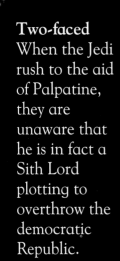

Two-faced
When the Jedi rush to the aid of Palpatine, they are unaware that he is in fact a Sith Lord plotting to overthrow the democratic Republic.

The space battle above Naboo was just the beginning. Worse was yet to come. A full-scale war broke out between the Republic and the droid armies. Their battle fleets met in a gigantic space conflict above Coruscant. The leader of the Republic, Supreme Chancellor Palpatine, had been kidnapped, and two Jedi set off to rescue him: Obi-Wan Kenobi and Anakin Skywalker.

Direct hit
Both sides lose some of their spaceships in the explosive space battle above Coruscant.

The Jedi dodged enemy fire and landed on the cruiser in which Palpatine was being held. After freeing Palpatine, Anakin had to pilot the cruiser to a crash landing after a Republic ship tore it apart.

Tiny but deadly
Small buzz droids attach themselves to the side of Obi-Wan's ship to inflict damage with their cutting arms.

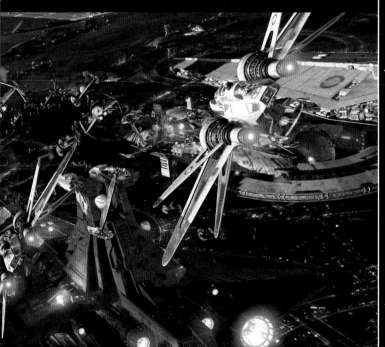

Deadly sky
Republic warships engage droid fighters large and small in the raging battle above Coruscant.

Some space battles involved many ships, like the battle above Coruscant. In others, just two ships engaged in a duel called a dogfight. When Obi-Wan was on the trail of a dangerous villain called Jango Fett, the chase led into a highly lethal asteroid field. Any collision with these floating rocks would be fatal. Jango tried to lose Obi-Wan by blasting rocks close to the Jedi's ship.

Distinctive ship
Jango pilots one of the deadliest ships in the galaxy, *Slave I*. It is armed with weapons and lethal surprises.

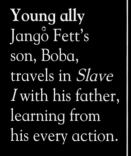

Young ally
Jango Fett's son, Boba, travels in *Slave I* with his father, learning from his every action.

Obi-Wan was a skilled pilot and he dodged each explosion. Then Jango steered his ship around an asteroid so he was now the one pursuing Obi-Wan. He fired a special seeker missile, but Obi-Wan faked his ship's explosion. When Jango saw the blast, he believed that Obi-Wan had been killed, but the clever Jedi was really hiding on one of the asteroids.

On the tail
Seeker missiles can home in on fast-moving objects so they are hard to shake off.

Jedi pilot
Even though Obi-Wan says he is not keen on flying, his piloting skills are superb.

Trusty ship
The *Falcon* is battle scarred from its many space adventures.

Another ship that has been in many dogfights is the *Millennium Falcon*. Piloted by Han Solo and Chewbacca, the ship could outrun most enemy craft. If the going got tough, the *Falcon* could jump to lightspeed, enabling it to vanish instantly and reappear somewhere far away.

Under pressure
A giant Star Destroyer chases the *Falcon* while Imperial TIE-fighters blast it with laser fire.

Heat of battle
Piloted by Han's old friend and rival, Lando Calrissian, the *Falcon* evades Imperial fighters at the second Death Star.

Hot shot
Han Solo was once a reckless smuggler. Then he joined the Rebel Alliance and eventually he even married Princess Leia.

Han Solo flew the *Falcon* in many daring raids against the Imperial fleet. Once, he landed right on the hull of an enormous Imperial Star Destroyer to evade its radar. Another time, he made the seemingly suicidal decision to fly into an asteroid field to shake off Imperial fighters. The daring plan worked and he escaped with his life.

Rebel space battles

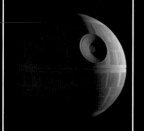

Death Star
The moon-sized Death Star had the firepower to destroy an entire planet.

Strike force
Rebel teams of X-wing and Y-wing starfighter pilots fly from their base on Yavin 4 toward the Death Star.

The Rebel Alliance was dedicated to opposing the oppressive rule of the Empire, despite being desperately under-equipped. The Empire had a massive starfleet, but the Alliance made do with a small number of battle-worn starfighters.

The Alliance learned that the Empire had built an enormous battle station called the Death Star. Stolen plans showed a flaw: If a Rebel starfighter could fire a torpedo into a tiny exhaust port, the chain reaction would destroy the battle station.

The Rebel pilots boldly launched an assault on the Death Star from their base on the planet Yavin 4. The Empire was not expecting an attack on its deadly superweapon. One Rebel pilot was skilled enough to strike the target: Luke Skywalker. The Death Star exploded—and the Rebels scored their first major victory against the Empire.

Enemy ships
Two Imperial ships chase the Rebel pilots along a narrow trench on the Death Star.

Hot shot
Luke hits the exhaust port that leads into the heart of the battle station's colossal reactor.

Rebel leader
Admiral Ackbar
is the loyal
Commander
of the Rebel
fleet at the
Battle of Endor.

*The battle rages
around the half-
completed
Death Star.*

The Battle of Endor was the final showdown between the Rebels and the Empire. Part of the conflict took place above the forest moon of Endor, where the Empire was building a second Death Star. While a team of Rebels landed on Endor's moon to disable the shield generator protecting the Death Star, the entire Rebel fleet came out of hiding to launch a final, do-or-die attack.

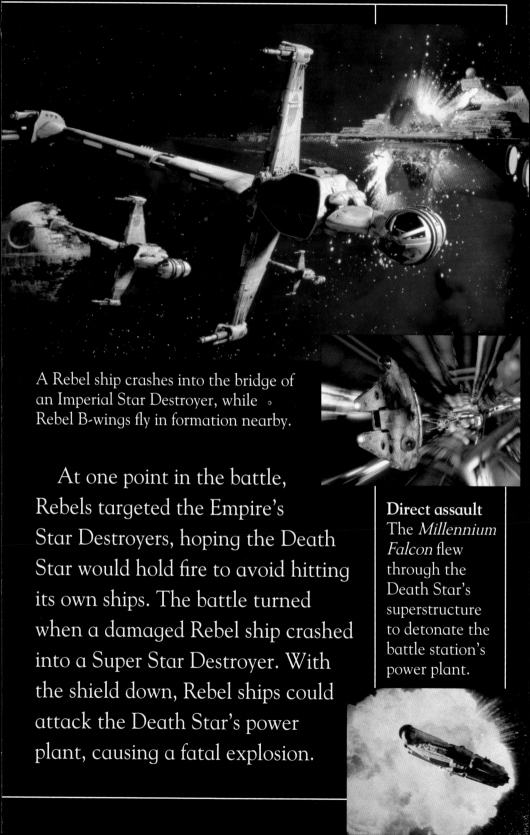

A Rebel ship crashes into the bridge of an Imperial Star Destroyer, while Rebel B-wings fly in formation nearby.

At one point in the battle, Rebels targeted the Empire's Star Destroyers, hoping the Death Star would hold fire to avoid hitting its own ships. The battle turned when a damaged Rebel ship crashed into a Super Star Destroyer. With the shield down, Rebel ships could attack the Death Star's power plant, causing a fatal explosion.

Direct assault
The *Millennium Falcon* flew through the Death Star's superstructure to detonate the battle station's power plant.

Lightsaber clashes

Since ancient times, the lightsaber has been the chosen weapon of the Jedi Knights. Until the Sith emerged from hiding, the Jedi used their lightsabers only as defence against blasters and other weapons. But the Sith also used lightsabers. Now the Jedi faced opponents armed with their own traditional weapon.

Surprise attack
Darth Maul first appears on the desert planet Tatooine. He ambushes Jedi Qui-Gon Jinn.

Sith opponent
On Naboo, it takes two skilled Jedi to hold back Darth Maul's double-bladed lightsaber.

*Obi-Wan leaps to avoid a low
parry from Maul's glowing blade.*

Final strike
Qui-Gon meets
Maul in a clash
that would spell
the Jedi's doom.

During the Battle of Naboo,
Darth Sidious's Sith apprentice,
Darth Maul, emerged. Maul's
appearance was terrifying, with face
tattoos, yellow eyes, and several
horns. Darth Maul attacked Jedi
Qui-Gon Jinn and Obi-Wan Kenobi.
He managed to kill Qui-Gon. Obi-
Wan was devastated but he fought
on until he had defeated his Sith foe.

Jedi in trouble
On the edge of
a deep shaft,
Maul nearly
triumphs over
Obi-Wan. But
the Jedi will not
give up until he
has defeated the
savage Sith.

Sith blade
Dooku's lightsaber blade is red, as all Sith blades are.

Captured Jedi
On Geonosis, Count Dooku wants Obi-Wan Kenobi to join him as a Sith.

With Darth Maul dead, Sith Lord Darth Sidious had to train a new apprentice. He chose a former Jedi called Count Dooku. The elegant, commanding Dooku left the Jedi Order to become a Sith. Sidious taught him to use the destructive dark side of the Force.

At the Battle of Geonosis, Dooku fought a great Jedi Master, Yoda. They clashed in a blur of lightsaber blows. Dooku used the Force to throw massive objects. This time, he managed to escape.

Jedi against Sith
The Jedi fight Dooku
onboard the cruiser.

Dooku next
faced Obi-Wan
and Anakin on
the cruiser where
Palpatine (really Darth
Sidious) was being held prisoner.
Dooku knocked Obi-Wan
unconscious. But he was unaware of
Sidious's masterplan: He wanted
Anakin to kill Dooku and replace
him as his new Sith apprentice.

Bad influence
Palpatine
encourages
Anakin to reject
his Jedi training
and unleash his
anger to kill
Dooku in
cold blood.

Count Dooku was not the only lightsaber-wielding foe the Jedi would meet during the Clone Wars. They also confronted a half-machine, half-living creature called Grievous, who was general of the droid armies. Grievous had also been trained by Count Dooku in lightsaber combat. He liked to steal lightsabers from the Jedi he killed, and hoped to add Obi-Wan and Anakin's weapons to his collection.

Lethal general
On Utapau, Obi-Wan finds that General Grievous is a dangerous opponent in lightsaber combat.

Utapau chase
Grievous on his wheelbike and Obi-Wan on a fast varactyl lizard trade blows on the planet Utapau.

Furious foe
Grievous's two arms can split into four, giving the Jedi extra lightsabers to dodge and parry. Obi-Wan will shear off some of these extra limbs.

But not this time! The daring Jedi fought off Grievous's bodyguards and escaped the general's clutches.

Grievous next met Obi-Wan on the planet Utapau. Wielding four lightsabers, Grievous unleashed a brutal assault. A high-speed chase across the planet surface led to a final showdown—and Grievous's dramatic demise in a ball of fire.

Explosive end
Obi-Wan uses a blaster to fire the fatal shots that enflame Grievous.

Lost cause
On the volcano planet called Mustafar, Obi-Wan realizes that Anakin is no longer a Jedi.

Sith opponent
Anakin, now named Darth Vader, unleashes his Sith powers against Obi-Wan Kenobi.

Ever since Senator Palpatine first met Anakin Skywalker, he knew the young Jedi had great powers. He also perceived Anakin's unruly emotions and knew he could be turned to the Sith cause. After he had encouraged Anakin to kill Dooku, Palpatine revealed that he was a Sith, and Anakin joined him, becoming Darth Vader. Then Palpatine made Vader believe Obi-Wan was against him.

Anakin's eyes gleam with anger as Obi-Wan defeats him in battle.

Darth Vader and Obi-Wan fought on the volcano planet Mustafar. Obi-Wan gained the upper hand and left Vader for dead. But Emperor Palpatine rebuilt Vader in black armor. Then Vader took his place beside the Emperor.

Darth Vader fought Obi-Wan once more, taking the Jedi's life. It wasn't until he battled with his own son that Vader was able to reject the Sith and the dark side.

Deadly rematch Vader and Obi-Wan meet in combat for the last time on the first Death Star.

Father-son duel Vader wants his son Luke to join him as a Sith, but Luke refused.

Cruel Master
Palpatine enjoys the fight between his Sith accomplice, Dooku, and his accomplice-to-be, Anakin.

Sith unmasked
Palpatine displays his Sith lightsaber skills in the fight with Mace Windu.

For a long time, the most evil Sith Lord in the galaxy went by the name of Palpatine. Pretending to be a friend to the Republic, he secretly masterminded a war that made him the cruel ruler of the galaxy.

The Jedi realized too late that Palpatine was really a Sith Lord named Darth Sidious. High-ranking Jedi Master Mace Windu lost his life attempting to stop the Sith schemer.

Palpatine had hidden his Sith lightsaber until Mace confronted him.

Even Yoda was unable to defeat the Emperor in lightsaber combat. In the end, Sidious's own ally, Darth Vader, sided with Vader's son, Luke Skywalker. Vader turned against his Sith Master and threw Emperor Palpatine to his death.

Explosive clash
The two most powerful users of the Force's light and dark sides clash in a spectacular duel in the Senate building on Coruscant.

Lightning strike
Sidious fires deadly Sith lightning at Luke. But Vader will be unable to stand by and let his son die.

Famous showdowns

Jango finds that
Obi-Wan is hard
to hit with a blaster.

Airborne foe
Jango uses his
jetpack to soar
above Obi-Wan
on Kamino.

Final end
In the arena
battle on
Geonosis, Jedi
Mace Windu
strikes the fatal
blow that ends
Jango's life.

Even before the Clone Wars, the
galaxy was not entirely peaceful.
Many criminals thrived, including
bounty hunters, who captured or
attacked people for a price. The best
bounty hunter in the galaxy was
named Jango Fett. Jango wore sleek
armor and carried many
weapons. He clashed with
Obi-Wan on a watery
planet called Kamino.

Though Jango escaped, the Battle of Geonosis would be his undoing. In the combat, Mace Windu struck Jango down with a powerful thrust from his lightsaber blade.

Jango's son Boba witnessed his father's death. Boba became a bounty hunter like his father. He came to work for Darth Vader and the notorious gangster Jabba the Hutt, among others. With Vader's help, Boba captured Han Solo and delivererd him to Jabba, who wanted Han for unpaid debts. A fierce battle ensued when Luke Skywalker and his friends rescued Solo from Jabba.

Battle-scarred
Boba Fett had many famous showdowns in his career as a bounty hunter. But he meets his match in the battle at Jabba's palace.

Deadly duel
Boba clashes with Luke, but a lucky strike from Han will knock the bounty hunter out of the battle.

Enter the beast
The three-horned reek enters the arena on Geonosis for a showdown with the human prisoners.

Jedi Knights, Rebels, and other defenders of freedom in the galaxy have had many showdowns with bounty hunters, assassins, and vile gangsters. They have also faced some nightmarish beasts.

On the planet Geonosis, Obi-Wan, Anakin, and Padmé Amidala were sentenced to public execution—by savage beasts.

Bared teeth
A soldier prods the nexu into the arena with a spear, where it bears its fangs in anticipation of fresh meat.

Obi-Wan faces the fearsome acklay in the Geonosis arena.

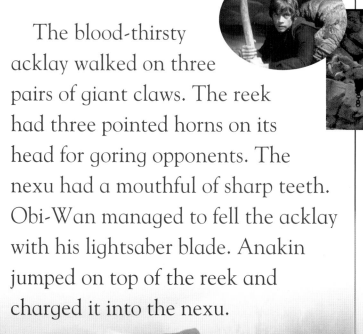

The blood-thirsty
acklay walked on three
pairs of giant claws. The reek
had three pointed horns on its
head for goring opponents. The
nexu had a mouthful of sharp teeth.
Obi-Wan managed to fell the acklay
with his lightsaber blade. Anakin
jumped on top of the reek and
charged it into the nexu.

Rancor beast
In Jabba's
palace, a caged
beast called a
rancor is let
loose upon Luke
Skywalker, but
proves no match
for the new Jedi.

Jabba's death
The massive
slug-like
gangster Jabba
the Hutt meets
an untimely end
at the hands of
Princess Leia.

A new era

At last—victory for the Rebel Alliance! The deaths of Emperor Palpatine and Darth Vader, and the destruction of the second Death Star, meant that the Empire was doomed. Peace and justice would soon be restored to the galaxy. The good news spread quickly and people rejoiced.

Father and son reunited
Luke looks at his father's true face for the first time, revealed beneath Darth Vader's helmet.

Forest celebration
In Endor's forests, Rebels and Ewoks celebrate the destruction of the terrible second Death Star that had threatened all of their lives.

The Rebel Alliance established a New Republic to replace the Empire. But troubles continued. Hundreds of planets that had accepted the Emperor's rule needed to be won over. Many loyal Imperial officers continued to attack the New Republic with remnants of the Imperial fleet. For Luke Skywalker, Han Solo, Princess Leia, and their allies, a new era had begun but the epic battle was not over yet.

Good times
Above the gigantic skyscrapers on Coruscant, fireworks light up the skies in celebration of the defeat of the evil Empire.

STAR WARS™
ULTIMATE DUELS

Written by Lindsay Kent

What is a duel?

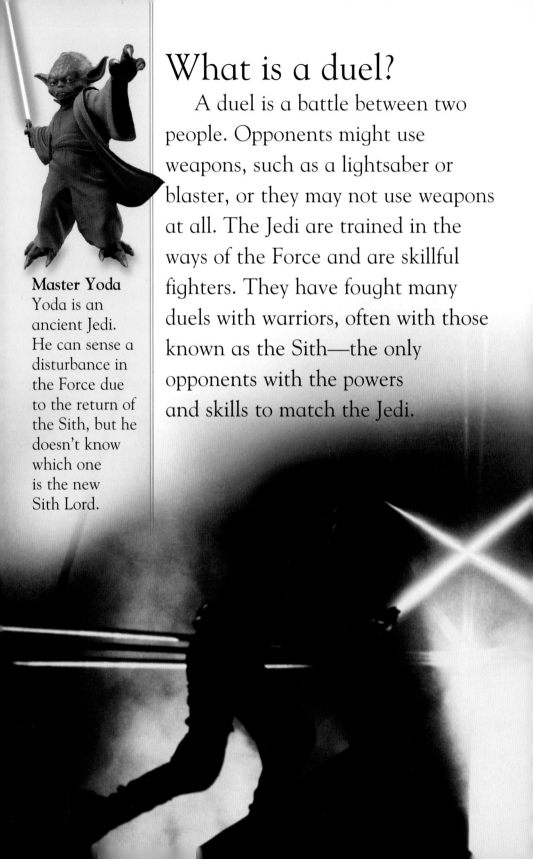

A duel is a battle between two people. Opponents might use weapons, such as a lightsaber or blaster, or they may not use weapons at all. The Jedi are trained in the ways of the Force and are skillful fighters. They have fought many duels with warriors, often with those known as the Sith—the only opponents with the powers and skills to match the Jedi.

Master Yoda
Yoda is an ancient Jedi. He can sense a disturbance in the Force due to the return of the Sith, but he doesn't know which one is the new Sith Lord.

The Sith are trained in the dark side of the Force but were thought to be extinct. The Sith are far from extinct. They are in hiding, waiting for the right moment to return and wreak revenge on the Jedi. With the return of their old enemy, the Jedi have many more duels to fight!

Sith Lord
Darth Sidious is the new powerful Sith Lord. For years he manages to keep his Sith identity secret by pretending to be a politician.

Jedi Knight Luke Skywalker fights Sith Lord Darth Vader in an epic battle.

A lightsaber can easily cut through durasteel blast doors.

Weapons

The most common weapon used by a Jedi in a duel is a lightsaber. A lightsaber is an elegant weapon. The user must be well-trained in the ways of the Force in order to wield it skillfully in combat. Every lightsaber is made to suit the owner's needs and preferences. It is held like a sword, but instead of a metal blade, a lightsaber has a beam of energy that bursts from the handle when the weapon is ignited.

Crystal
A crystal is placed inside the handle of each lightsaber. The crystal focuses the energy released from a power cell and the blade of energy is produced.

Crystal placed inside

Lightsaber handle

A lightsaber can cut through most things, but not the blade of another lightsaber. The weapon is used like a sword in combat, but a lightsaber can have other important uses. Jedi can use the Force to predict incoming energy bolts from blaster guns and use a lightsaber to deflect the bolts back toward their opponent.

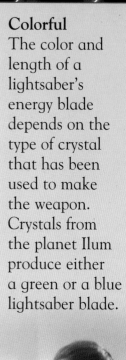

Colorful
The color and length of a lightsaber's energy blade depends on the type of crystal that has been used to make the weapon. Crystals from the planet Ilum produce either a green or a blue lightsaber blade.

A Sith apprentice called Darth Maul favors a double-bladed lightsaber, as it suits his style of combat.

At one with the Force
Even during battle and situations of extreme stress, a Jedi tries to remain calm and focused.

Jedi training

The Jedi Order is an ancient peacekeeping organization. The Jedi use the Force to defend and to protect others, so it is important that they learn to fight skillfully in a duel. It takes years to become a Jedi so training usually begins at a very early age. Younglings are taught to use lightsabers. At times their eyes are covered while they train so they can learn to feel the Force and use their instincts, instead of relying on what they can see.

Trainees also learn how to use the Force to move objects without physically touching them. A Force pull enables Jedi to bring something to them. A Force push is a powerful technique that can repel objects or opponents.

Jedi Master Qui-Gon Jinn performs a Force push to repel several droids.

A Jedi novice learns to live by the Jedi Code—a set of rules the Jedi obey. According to the Code, the Jedi must use the Force for good. They should have compassion for all life, and must engage in combat only in defense of others or themselves.

Fighting fit
Jedi Knights are experts in using lightsabers but they must also be physically strong and fit. Yoda teaches a young Jedi, named Luke Skywalker, to be agile.

The Sith always come in pairs— a Master and an apprentice. Knowledge of the dark side of the Force is passed on from Master to apprentice.

Sith methods

Like the Jedi, the Sith are able to sense and use the Force when they duel. The Sith's Force training, however, varies greatly from that of the Jedi. They use the dark side of the Force and gain their power from raw emotions, such as anger, pain, and hatred. The Sith do not value life or feel compassion, and their ferocious style of combat reflects their attitudes.

The Sith act in aggression and not in defense, and feel free to do anything in battle—no matter how devious.

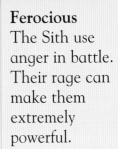

The Sith can use the Force to produce Force lightning. They channel the Force through their bodies and discharge powerful bolts of energy from their palms and fingertips into their opponents. The Sith can also use the Force to choke a victim without actually touching them.

Ferocious
The Sith use anger in battle. Their rage can make them extremely powerful.

A Sith Lord named Darth Vader often uses the Force choke on opponents.

A forgotten menace

The Jedi first meet their old enemy, the Sith, on a planet called Tatooine. Jedi Master Qui-Gon Jinn is escorting Queen Amidala to Coruscant when a Sith named Darth Maul arrives on a speeder bike, and begins a fierce attack on Qui-Gon. The mysterious assailant fights with a double-bladed lightsaber. It is clear that he is highly trained in the ways of the Force. He battles the Jedi Master with incredible skill and power.

Qui-Gon struggles to cope with Maul's surprising skills and only narrowly escapes when Queen Amidala's starship picks him up. The Jedi is unprepared for the encounter because the Sith were believed to be extinct. It is clear from this duel that the Sith are very much alive and more powerful than ever.

Qui-Gon Jinn
Qui-Gon Jinn is an experienced Jedi Master. He was taught by a Jedi called Count Dooku.

A new Sith
Darth Maul is Darth Sidious' apprentice. His entire body is covered in tattoos revealing his origins as a Nightbrother of Dathomir.

Duels on Naboo

Obi-Wan Kenobi
Obi-Wan is a skilled and dedicated Jedi. When he cuts Darth Maul in half, he becomes the first Jedi in centuries to defeat a Sith in battle.

Qui-Gon Jinn and his apprentice, Obi-Wan Kenobi, encounter Darth Maul again on Naboo. Maul fights both Jedi at once until Obi-Wan becomes separated from Qui-Gon and the Sith. Qui-Gon is no match for Maul and he is fatally injured. Obi-Wan is upset and angry, and his raw emotions take him toward the dark side of the Force for a time, but he manages to calm himself.

As Obi-Wan and Maul fight, it is clear that the Sith is more powerful. Maul uses the Force to push Obi-Wan over the edge of a pit, leaving the Jedi hanging from a pipe. Darth Maul believes victory will be his and smiles and taunts his opponent. He kicks Obi-Wan's lightsaber into the pit, but the Jedi uses the Force to retrieve Qui-Gon's weapon. In a surprise move, Obi-Wan jumps out of the pit and strikes Maul with one swift blow.

Arrogance
Darth Maul is over-confident and so he underestimates Obi-Wan. This leads to his downfall.

Conflict on Kamino

Clone Army
The clones are exact copies of Jango Fett but they grow much faster than a normal human. This allows the Kaminoans to produce thousands of soldiers in a short time.

Obi-Wan travels to a water planet called Kamino where he discovers that the Kaminoans have been creating a huge clone army. The army was supposedly ordered by a Jedi called Sifo-Dyas, but Obi-Wan learns that the Jedi Council doesn't know about the army. Every soldier is a copy of a bounty hunter called Jango Fett.

When Obi-Wan meets Jango, the bounty hunter tries to escape, and he and Obi-Wan begin a violent brawl.

Jango can't use the Force, but his suit contains many gadgets, and these give him an advantage when Obi-Wan loses his lightsaber.

Jango binds Obi-Wan's hands together with his wrist-mounted wire and Obi-Wan falls over the edge of a landing platform. Jango is dragged down, too, but just in time he manages to cut the wire and escapes on his starship *Slave I.*

Jango Fett
Jango Fett is one of the most successful bounty hunters in the galaxy. His special suit is fitted with weapons such as wrist blades and blaster pistols. It also has a jetpack.

Anakin Skywalker
Anakin is one of the most gifted Jedi to ever live. He was a slave before he joined the Jedi Order and became Obi-Wan's apprentice.

Darth Tyranus
Count Dooku is lured to the dark side of the Force by Darth Sidious. Dooku becomes the Sith Lord's apprentice, Darth Tyranus.

Battle of Geonosis

On the rocky planet of Geonosis the Jedi must fight another Sith opponent. Jedi Knight Obi-Wan Kenobi and his Padawan, Anakin Skywalker, discover that a once-respected Jedi, Count Dooku, has turned to the dark side. Obi-Wan and Anakin must stop Dooku from escaping.

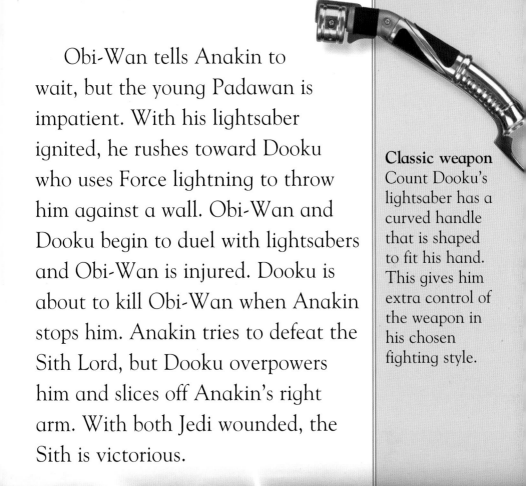

Obi-Wan tells Anakin to wait, but the young Padawan is impatient. With his lightsaber ignited, he rushes toward Dooku who uses Force lightning to throw him against a wall. Obi-Wan and Dooku begin to duel with lightsabers and Obi-Wan is injured. Dooku is about to kill Obi-Wan when Anakin stops him. Anakin tries to defeat the Sith Lord, but Dooku overpowers him and slices off Anakin's right arm. With both Jedi wounded, the Sith is victorious.

Classic weapon
Count Dooku's lightsaber has a curved handle that is shaped to fit his hand. This gives him extra control of the weapon in his chosen fighting style.

Concern for others
Dooku exploits the fact that the Jedi value all life. He knows Yoda will choose to save Anakin and Obi-Wan rather than letting them die in order to capture Dooku.

Obi-Wan and Anakin lie injured in Dooku's secret hangar when another Jedi enters—Master Yoda. Count Dooku uses Force power to hurl objects at Yoda, and causes sections of the ceiling to fall on him. Yoda defends himself, diverting the missiles away by using his own Force powers. Yoda and Dooku then fight with lightsabers. In spite of his age Yoda shows amazing athletic abilities.

Dooku is unable to defeat Yoda, and is in danger of being captured. Dooku distracts him by endangering Obi-Wan and Anakin. He uses the Force to drop an enormous pillar toward the injured pair. Dooku knows Yoda will need all of his power to save them, so he is able to slip away in his Solar Sailer.

Rescuing Palpatine

When the Trade Federation appears to kidnap Chancellor Palpatine, Jedi Knights Obi-Wan and Anakin are sent to rescue him. Once again they must face their old foe, Count Dooku. Obi-Wan is knocked unconscious with a powerful Force push by the Sith, but this time Anakin isn't so easy to overpower.

Devious Chancellor Palpatine pretends that he has been kidnapped. He wants Dooku and Anakin to fight so that Anakin can defeat Dooku and become Palpatine's new apprentice.

Count Dooku throws Obi-Wan across the room with a Force push.

Dooku goads Anakin during their fight. He believes he still has the advantage, but he is suddenly outmaneuvered by Anakin, who severs both of Dooku's hands. Unable to fight, Dooku falls to his knees before Anakin. On Palpatine's command, Anakin kills Dooku.

Dishonorable
Killing someone who is hurt and weak is not the Jedi way. Anakin's decision to kill Dooku takes him much closer to the dark side—just as Palpatine hopes it will.

Battle of Utapau

After the failed attempt to kidnap Chancellor Palpatine, the Jedi Council sends Obi-Wan on a mission to hunt down General Grievous. Palpatine believes that the Clone Wars cannot end until Grievous is captured. Obi-Wan travels to Utapau where he finds Grievous in one of the planet's large sinkhole cities.

Grievous is part-living creature and part-droid, which makes him a difficult opponent to beat.

Sinkhole city
The planet of Utapau is covered in deep holes, known as sinkholes. The Utapaun people have built cities in these holes.

He has four artificial arms, which enable him to wield four lightsabers at once with brute force and speed.

Although Grievous has been trained in lightsaber combat he cannot use the Force like Obi-Wan. The Jedi is able to anticipate Grievous' blows and cuts off several of the cyborg's hands, forcing him to flee.

General Grievous
Grievous was one of the greatest military leaders on the planet of Kalee until he was fatally injured in a shuttle crash. He was then rebuilt as a cyborg.

Varactyls
Utapau is home to giant bird-like lizards called varactyls. The creatures are used for transport as they are agile and have huge claws so they can grip the stone sides of the sinkholes.

Grievous escapes on his wheel bike, pursued by Obi-Wan on a varactyl named Boga. Obi-Wan loses his lightsaber during the chase, but manages to grab Grievous' electrostaff and the duel continues. The cyborg has the advantage because he is very strong and has an armored body, and Obi-Wan is nearly beaten. The Jedi is knocked over the edge of a landing platform and hangs precariously above a vast chasm.

Just as Grievous approaches, armed with his electrostaff, Obi-Wan uses the Force to grab Grievous' pistol and blasts his opponent. Normally the plates that protect Grievous' internal organs would have deflected the blast, but during the brawl Obi-Wan had managed to loosen the plates, so the shot kills the General.

Deadly weapon
Grievous' guards use weapons called electrostaffs. They are made of a very strong material that does not break even after being struck by a lightsaber blade. Each end of a staff emits deadly levels of energy.

Darth Sidious
Anakin
discovers that
Palpatine is
really Darth
Sidious—the
Sith Lord for
which the Jedi
have been
searching.

A Sith Lord revealed

When Chancellor Palpatine's true identity as a Sith Lord is revealed to Anakin, Jedi Master Mace Windu goes to the Senate to arrest him. Mace is accompanied by three other Jedi, but they are caught off-guard when the Chancellor suddenly ignites a lightsaber and attacks them. Within seconds he kills everyone except Windu.

Mace Windu
Jedi Master
Mace Windu is
a senior member
of the Jedi
Council. He is
experienced,
wise, and
well-respected
by other
Jedi.

The Jedi Master and Palpatine engage in a fierce lightsaber duel. Windu manages to disarm Palpatine, but the Sith uses the dark side to bombard Windu with Force lightning.

Windu deflects the lightning back toward Palpatine with his lightsaber, causing Palpatine's face to become scarred. Windu is about to finish off Palpatine when Anakin steps in and cuts off Windu's hand that was holding his lightsaber. Palpatine seizes the opportunity to attack Windu, using more Force lightning to throw the Jedi through the window to his death.

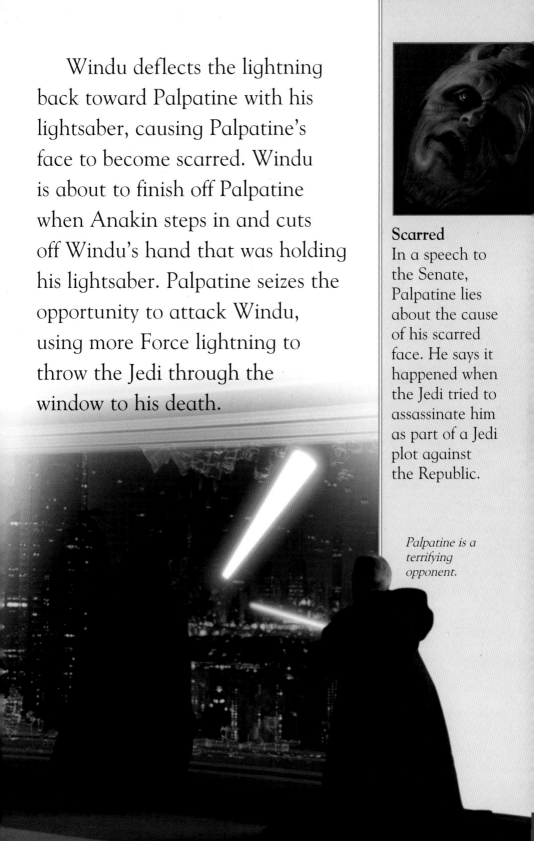

Scarred
In a speech to the Senate, Palpatine lies about the cause of his scarred face. He says it happened when the Jedi tried to assassinate him as part of a Jedi plot against the Republic.

Palpatine is a terrifying opponent.

Close contest

As Supreme Chancellor Palpatine becomes more powerful within the Republic, the Jedi are in grave danger. Palpatine commands the Clone Army to carry out Order 66—exterminate the Jedi. Most Jedi are killed, but Yoda survives. He then goes to the Senate to face Darth Sidious.

Sidious uses Force lightning to throw Yoda across his office. It appears that he is too strong for the Jedi Master, who lies motionless. The Sith Lord gloats about his apparent victory, but Yoda surprises him with a powerful Force push.

Royal Guards
Sidious' Royal Guards are well-trained, but they are no match for Yoda. The Jedi defeats them using the Force with just a small movement of his hands.

Yoda and Sidious begin a frenzied lightsaber duel and the two highly skilled Masters are evenly matched. Still fighting, they mount the Senate speaking platform that begins to rise, lifting the two opponents into the Senate Chamber.

Emperor's podium
The ceiling of Palpatine's office opens up and the speaking platform rises into the Senate Chamber. Standing on the podium, Palpatine declares himself to be Emperor.

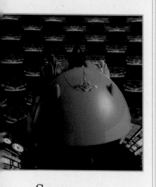

Senate Chamber
The chamber is the largest room in the Senate Building on Coruscant. Within the chamber are thousands of pods. Each pod holds Senators from all over the galaxy.

Both Yoda and Sidious are powerful, and as their lightsaber duel continues in the Senate Chamber, it is clear that neither is able to defeat the other easily. Sidious uses the Force to launch huge Senate pods at Yoda, which causes the Jedi to drop his lightsaber. Yoda gains the upper hand when he pushes a pod back at Sidious, who falls. However, the Sith is able to grab hold of a pod and clambers to safety.

Sidious uses brutal Force lightning again and Yoda deflects it back, but the counterblow throws him over the edge of the pod and down to the chamber floor. Yoda is not badly hurt, but he realizes that he cannot defeat Sidious this time and decides to flee.

Escape
Yoda escapes thanks to Bail Organa who picks him up in his airspeeder. Yoda then travels to a planet called Dagobah where he hides from the Emperor for many years.

Evenly matched
Vader and Obi-Wan try to Force push each other, and they are both repelled across the chamber.

Master and apprentice

It is with sorrow that Obi-Wan learns that Anakin has succumbed to the dark side of the Force. He has become Sidious' new apprentice and is now called Darth Vader. Obi-Wan goes to the volcano planet of Mustafar to confront his old apprentice, and finds Vader in a lava mining facility. Obi-Wan tries to reason with Vader, but it is clear that he has lost his friend to Sidious.

Vader and Obi-Wan ignite their lightsabers and begin an intense battle. Vader is consumed with rage and hatred, and the duel is brutal. During the fight the shields protecting the mining facility from the lava are shut down, and the entire structure begins to melt into a river of molten lava. With Obi-Wan on a lava skiff and Vader on a droid, the former friends continue their fight, hovering above the lava.

Sadness
Obi-Wan is distraught at having to fight his apprentice and friend. Anakin had been like a brother to him.

Flaming rivers
Lava rivers flow all over Mustafar. The lava bursts from beneath the planet's surface like huge fiery fountains. The skies above Mustafar are always dark because they are filled with black clouds of ash and smoke.

As Obi-Wan and Vader approach a riverbank, Obi-Wan manages to jump off the lava skiff onto a high slope. He sees that Vader is about to do the same, and warns him not to, as he has the higher ground. Vader is arrogant and doesn't listen. He leaps toward Obi-Wan, allowing the Jedi Master to perform a final winning blow, and Vader is defeated.

Obi-Wan cannot bring himself to kill his former comrade, however, and so he leaves him there. Darth Sidious senses Vader's plight and flies to Mustafar where he finds his new apprentice barely alive. He then uses his dark powers to save him. Medical droids reconstruct Vader's body using robotic parts and encase the Sith in a black suit that allows him to breathe.

The Emperor and Darth Vader are a fearsome pair. The Emperor has complete control over the Galactic Empire. With Vader by his side, there is no one with the courage or the ability to challenge him.

Reconstruction
Medical droids use advanced technology to rebuild Darth Vader's body. There is little left of the man who was once Anakin Skywalker. Vader is now more machine than man.

Death Star
The Death Star is a huge space station, built by the Emperor. The Death Star has a weapon that is so powerful it can destroy an entire planet.

Death Star duel

On the Imperial Death Star, Obi-Wan Kenobi and Darth Vader meet again after many years. Since the Emperor seized power, Obi-Wan has been in hiding, living a simple, solitary life, but all that is about to change. A member of the Rebel Alliance named Princess Leia is captured by Imperial troops and asks for Obi-Wan's help.

Darth Vader immediately senses Obi-Wan's presence on the Death Star and goes to face him. They fight with lightsabers as before, but the duel is very different from their last encounter. Obi-Wan is older and weaker, and sees that Vader is too strong for him. But beating his former apprentice is not part of his plan. Obi-Wan knows that if he sacrifices himself he will become one with the Force and more powerful, so he allows Vader to kill him.

Force Ghost
After death, some Jedi, like Obi-Wan Kenobi, are able to use the Force to talk to the living and advise them. These Jedi are called Force Ghosts.

87

Cloud City clash

The duel on Cloud City is between Darth Vader and a young Jedi-in-training named Luke Skywalker. Before Luke can complete his training with Yoda, he rushes to Cloud City on Bespin, sensing that his friends Princess Leia, Han Solo, and Chewbacca are in danger. He doesn't realize that his friends' capture is part of a plan hatched by Vader to bring Luke to him.

Luke doesn't have enough experience to face Vader, and throughout the battle Vader uses his superior Force powers and lightsaber skills against him.

Vader's attack is relentless and in a final blow, he severs Luke's hand. Vader then reveals that he is Luke's father and tempts him with the power of the dark side. But Luke chooses to sacrifice himself rather than be corrupted and falls down a shaft. He is sucked into a chute, however, and ends up clinging to the underside of Cloud City until Princess Leia rescues him.

Father and son
Vader and the Emperor find out that Luke is the son of Anakin Skywalker— Vader's former self. Luke will be a powerful addition to the dark side if they can turn him.

Cunning plan
Luke's Jedi powers have grown strong and he has become wiser. When Luke confronts Jabba, he lets Jabba capture him—it is all part of his plan.

Jabba the Hutt
Jabba is a notorious crime lord, who lives on a desert planet called Tatooine. His legless body looks like a giant slug.

Battle of wits

Crime lord Jabba the Hutt has captured Luke Skywalker's friends Princess Leia, Han Solo, and Chewbacca, so Luke must free them. He goes to Jabba's palace and demands their release, but Jabba just laughs at him. Jabba doesn't physically fight Luke—he has his own methods! He opens a trapdoor and Luke falls into the rancor's den. The rancor creature is huge and ferocious, but Luke manages to defeat it.

Jabba then orders his guards to feed Luke and his friends to the Sarlacc. Jabba eagerly awaits Luke's death, but he doesn't know that Luke has hidden his lightsaber in his droid, R2-D2, who is on Jabba's sail barge.

The terrifying rancor is a huge reptile-like creature.

R2-D2 ejects the lightsaber toward Luke who then destroys Jabba's men. Thanks to the chaos Luke causes, the guards on Jabba's barge are distracted, giving Leia the chance to strangle Jabba. In the battle of wits between Luke and Jabba, the Jedi proves wiser.

The Sarlacc
Hidden beneath the desert sands of Tatooine is a creature called the Sarlacc. Its mouth is surrounded by tentacles that capture its prey.

Explosive!
Luke and his friends escape just as Jabba's sail barge explodes.

The Rebel Alliance obtains plans showing how to shut down the Death Star's defense shield, so it can be destroyed. They don't realize that the Death Star is already operational and extremely dangerous.

Final confrontation

The battle between Luke and the Emperor on the Death Star begins with words, not physical combat. When Luke arrives, the Emperor tries to tempt him to join the dark side. The Emperor tells Luke that it is his destiny and encourages Luke to give in to his anger and fight him. For a while Luke refuses to be provoked, but the Emperor senses how much Luke's Rebel friends mean to him and uses this to goad him.

The Emperor reveals that he knows that the Rebels plan to attack the Death Star and that he allowed false information about the Death Star to reach Rebel hands. The Emperor tells Luke that his Rebel friends are about to be destroyed; Luke cannot hold back his rage any longer. Luke sees his lightsaber next to the Emperor and draws it to him. He tries to strike the Emperor, but Vader stops him. Father and son then begin their final battle.

Over-confident
When Vader arrives with Luke, the Emperor sends his guards away. The Sith Lord believes that he is invincible and they will not be needed.

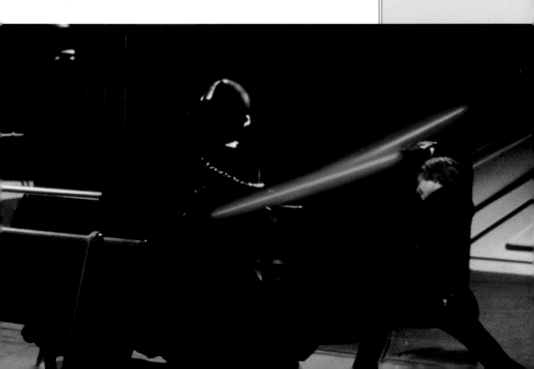

The Sith defeated
It appears that seeing Luke revives the former Jedi within Vader. When he decides to stop the Emperor, he turns away from the dark side of the Force.

Luke's anger and experience make him stronger than the last time he fought Vader. Now Luke has the upper hand and the opportunity to end Vader's life. Although he is tempted to kill Vader, Luke manages to control his rage. He refuses to kill his father and be turned to the dark side. Instead he throws down his lightsaber and surrenders.

The Emperor is surprised by Luke's strength of mind, but is furious that he will not join him. Enraged, the Emperor bombards Luke with Force lightning in a one-sided battle, clearly enjoying the pain he is causing Luke.

As Luke writhes in agony he begs his father to help him, but Vader looks on and does nothing. The Emperor is about to end the young Jedi's life, when Vader suddenly picks up his evil Master and throws him down a reactor shaft, killing him. By doing this he saves his son and destroys the Empire.

A machine no more
Vader has gone and Anakin Skywalker has returned, but because the Emperor's Force lightning has wounded him and damaged his suit, he cannot survive for long. His last wish is to see Luke through his own eyes.

The Emperor falls to his death.

STAR WARS

BEWARE THE DARK SIDE

Written by Simon Beecroft

Faces of Evil

A long time ago, the galaxy was ruled by an evil man named Darth Sidious (pronounced SID-EE-US). He was also known as Emperor Palpatine (pronounced PAL-PA-TEEN). He used fear, corruption, and the dark side of the Force to rule his evil Empire.

The Force
The Force is an invisible energy created by all living things. A few people with special powers can control the Force. The Force is mostly a good energy, but it also has a dark side that can be used for evil.

Emperor Palpatine

Darth Sidious's special abilities made him very powerful. He used the dark side of the Force to control people's minds and events. He also used the dark side to throw heavy objects with his mind, and to fire a deadly lightning from his fingers.

In these pages, you will meet many villains who used the dark side of the Force to do terrible things. You will also meet evildoers who did not use the Force, but who were still on the side of darkness. Finally, you will meet the brave few who dared to stand up to the dark side.

The Jedi order
Jedi Master Obi-Wan Kenobi said that the Force "surrounds us, penetrates us, and binds the galaxy together." The Jedi are a group of individuals who devote their lives to using the Force for good. The Jedi protect people and keep peace in the galaxy.

Sith lightsabers
Each Jedi builds his or her own weapon called a lightsaber. They are made from glowing energy crystals. Sith lightsaber blades are usually red.

Sith Lord

Darth Sidious was a Sith Lord. The Sith had been around for many centuries. The first Sith was a Jedi who turned to the dark side. Others followed him. Together they tried to destroy the Jedi. The Sith even tried to kill each other because they were so full of evil and hatred. The Jedi thought they had destroyed the Sith. But, one Sith survived. He took an apprentice and went into hiding. Since then, the Sith have plotted revenge on the Jedi.

The Sith were the Jedi's most feared enemies. The Sith used the dark side of the Force to gain terrible powers. Like the Jedi, they fought with a lightsaber, which is a sword whose blade is made of pure energy. The Sith and the Jedi were the only people in the galaxy who used lightsabers. The lightsaber was the ancient weapon of the Jedi, but since the Sith were once Jedi, they used them, too.

Lightsabers
The handle contains special crystals that make the energy blade appear when needed. Jedi lightsaber blades are either blue, green, or purple.

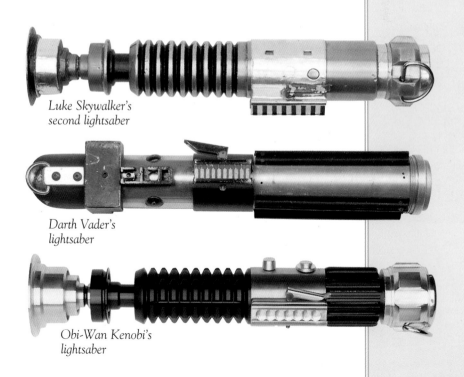

Luke Skywalker's second lightsaber

Darth Vader's lightsaber

Obi-Wan Kenobi's lightsaber

Sith Powers

The Sith believed that the dark side of the Force was more powerful than the light. Turning to the dark side seemed to bring results quickly, while the Jedi had to patiently study the light side of the Force for many years. The Sith also rejected the Jedi's teachings that emotions must be controlled. They used anger and hatred to become stronger, but the Sith had no loyalty and were often destroyed by the dark side.

Evil temptation
The Jedi understood that the dark side was a powerful temptation for all Jedi. Most managed to resist it, but a few gave in to its evil powers.

In battle, the Sith tried to crush their opponents with heavy objects, which they threw using their dark side energies.

The dark side of the Force gave the Sith powers that the Jedi did not have. One of them was deadly Force lightning. They could fire it from their fingers at an opponent. However, this power was very dangerous and could also harm the user.

Force lightning
When Sidious attacked a Jedi called Mace Windu with Force lightning, Mace threw it back at Sidious. The lightning hit Sidious's face and scarred it forever.

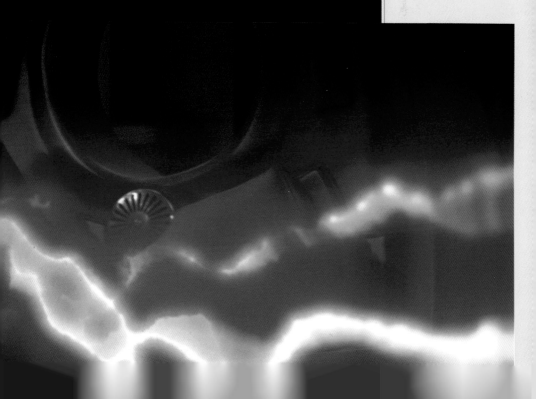

Galactic Republic
When the galaxy was united in peace, a Galactic Republic was formed. It was a democracy, which meant that every person in nearly all the worlds had a voice.

The Phantom Menace

Before Darth Sidious became Emperor of the galaxy, he was a popular politician called Senator Palpatine. At this time, the galaxy was at peace and laws were made in the Senate. All the different planets had a voice in the Senate and large armies were outlawed.

Palpatine secretly wanted to take over the galaxy. He planned to destroy the Senate and build a massive army so that he could force every planet to do what he wanted.

No one suspected that Palpatine was really a Sith Lord. After he secretly started a war in the galaxy, Palpatine convinced the Senate to make him their leader, the Supreme Chancellor. Then he gave himself the power to make all the decisions. Finally, he crowned himself Emperor. Now the dark side ruled the galaxy.

The Senate
The Senate was a gigantic circular building on the galaxy's capital planet, Coruscant.

Secret Sith
Palpatine hid his true Sith identity from the Senate.

Jedi Defenders

When the Sith revealed themselves after two thousand years in hiding, only the Jedi had the powers to face them. The Jedi vow to use their Force powers only to do good. The good side of the Force is known as the light side.

Learning to use the light side of the Force takes many years. Those who become Jedi begin training as young children. They must leave their families behind and live in the Jedi Temple on a big planet.

Yoda
Yoda was the wisest Jedi of all. He was hundreds of years old when the Sith reappeared.

The Jedi learn to control their emotions so that they can remain calm and practical in all situations. The Jedi seek to keep the Force in balance in the galaxy, which means that they must stop those who seek to use the dark side.

The Jedi can actually listen to the Force telling them that there is trouble happening somewhere. This is known as a disturbance in the Force. It means there is a problem some place in the galaxy—and the Jedi must find it and do whatever they can to stop it.

Obi-Wan
Obi-Wan Kenobi was a powerful Jedi. While the Sith ruled the galaxy, Obi-Wan went into hiding. Yoda also went into hiding.

Jedi Council
The wisest, most experienced Jedi sat on the Jedi High Council. Before the Sith attacked, Yoda felt great disturbances in the Force, but even he was not able to see where the threat came from.

Masked man
Vader's armor and breathing equipment were created in a secret medical facility.

Vader uncovered
Vader removed his helmet only in a special isolation chamber. Mechanical arms lifted the helmet from his scarred head.

Darth Vader

Darth Vader ruled the galaxy alongside Darth Sidious. Vader was also a Sith Lord. His knowledge of the dark side of the Force made him a powerful and dangerous figure. Vader would kill anyone who got in his way or disobeyed him, even his own generals. He used his Force powers to strangle people without even touching them.

Darth Vader always
wore a black suit of
armor and a black
mask because his body
had been almost
destroyed in a great
battle. His armor and mask
contained breathing equipment and
life-support systems to keep him
alive. The wheezing sound of
Vader's artificial breathing was
enough to strike terror into the
mind of anyone he approached.

Space fighter
Vader flew his
own fighter ship
into combat.
He was a very
daring pilot.

Lightsaber duel
Vader was a
merciless
opponent in
battle, and did
not hesitate to
cut down his
former Master,
Obi-Wan
Kenobi.

Anakin Skywalker

Boyhood
Anakin was born on a poor desert planet called Tatooine. He spent his boyhood as a slave until a Jedi Master named Qui-Gon Jinn rescued him.

Tragic death
When Anakin joined the Jedi, he had to leave his mother behind. He never forgave himself when he could not prevent her from dying at the hands of a vicious species called Sand People.

Before he became a Sith Lord, Darth Vader was a Jedi called Anakin Skywalker. Anakin was one of the most talented Jedi ever. His Force powers were incredibly strong, but Anakin was impatient. He wanted to become more powerful than any other Jedi.

Palpatine befriended Anakin and began to plant ideas in his mind. He convinced Anakin to join him on the dark side and train to be a Sith. Palpatine told Anakin that the dark side of the Force was more powerful than the light side. He even told Anakin that he would be able to stop his wife from dying. Anakin wanted this more than anything, so he rejected his Jedi training and joined Palpatine.

When Anakin joined the dark side, he killed many Jedi. He even fought his best friend, Obi-Wan Kenobi (pronounced OH-BEE-ONE KEN-OH-BEE). On the edge of a lava river, Anakin and Obi-Wan fought fiercely until Obi-Wan managed to strike down his former friend. Anakin fell near the lava and burst into flames. Palpatine rescued him, and re-built his badly burned body with robotic parts and a suit of armor—and Darth Vader was born!

Padmé Amidala
Anakin secretly married the Senator for Naboo, Padmé Amidala, even though the Jedi are forbidden to marry.

Darth Maul

Each Sith Master chose a single apprentice, whom he trained in the dark side. Sidious first chose a savage alien from the planet Iridonia. Given the Sith name Darth Maul, he served his master obediently, although he was only waiting for the day when he would take Sidious's place.

Maul had horns on his head and yellow eyes. His face was tattooed with dark side symbols. Maul used a double-bladed lightsaber.

Sith ship
Maul's spaceship could make itself appear invisible to others.

Speeder
Maul also used a speeder that flew along just above the ground. It had an open cockpit.

When two Jedi named Qui-Gon Jinn (pronounced KWY-GONN-JIN) and Obi-Wan Kenobi started to upset Sidious's plans, he sent Darth Maul to kill them. The fight took place on the edge of a giant power generator on Palpatine's home planet called Naboo. The Jedi were not prepared for such a ferocious attack. Qui-Gon Jinn was killed, but Obi-Wan Kenobi managed to defeat the deadly Sith apprentice.

Sith Master
Sidious kept in contact with his apprentice using a hologram transmitter.

Count Dooku

Sidious needed a new apprentice after Obi-Wan killed Darth Maul on Naboo. His search led him to Count Dooku, who was once a Jedi Master. Although he joined the Jedi order at a young age, Dooku was interested in the dark side and wanted power to change things quickly. When Dooku joined Sidious, he took the new Sith name— Darth Tyranus.

Weapon
Tyranus's weapon was a lightsaber with a curved handle. His special moves could surprise even the most experienced Jedi.

Count Dooku

For many years, Dooku had been encouraging planets and business organizations to leave the Senate and build droid armies. He told them that this would make the galaxy a better place. In reality he was doing only what Sidious told him to do. He did not know what Sidious's true plans were.

Force lightning
Like Sidious, Tyranus used Force lightning to deadly effect.

Sidious eventually betrayed Dooku and allowed him to be killed by Anakin Skywalker. Sidious knew that the powerful and gifted Anakin would be a more useful Sith apprentice than Dooku.

Droid Army

Count Dooku had persuaded many planets and organizations to buy powerful droid armies. The footsoldiers were blaster-wielding battle droids while heavily armored super battle droids provided backup. Hailfire droids rolled across the battlefields, each equipped with deadly cannon or missile launchers. Deadly machines called droideka were used on special missions.

Hailfire droids
Hailfire droids are shaped like massive wheels. They can race across flat ground or shallow lakes, flattening anything in their path.

Tri-fighters seek
out and hunt
down enemy
ships in space,
training their
deadly nose
cannons on
their prey.

Heavily armed droid ships were
also used for space battles. They
included vulture droids, which could
also walk along the ground, and
tri-fighters. Swarms of tiny buzz
droids attached themselves
to enemy ships. Although
they were very small,
their cutting and sawing
arms could inflict
serious damage.

Spider droid
Spider droids go
into battle
equipped with
heat-seeking
missiles.

General Grievous

With the outbreak of war in the galaxy, many brutal fiends joined the Sith Lords. One such recruit was General Grievous, a warlord whose battle-scarred body had been rebuilt with cyborg parts. The only parts of his original body left were his reptile-like eyes and his inner organs, which were protected by armor. Although he was more machine than man, Grievous would kill anyone who called him a droid.

Bodyguards
Grievous was accompanied by droid bodyguards, who were equipped with deadly energy staffs.

Grievous became Supreme
Commander of the droid armies.
Dooku taught Grievous to use
a lightsaber, although Grievous
could not use the Force like the
Sith and Jedi.

Grievous had a long-standing
grudge against the Jedi, and took
the lightsabers of any Jedi he killed.
In battle, Grievous could split his
two arms into four, each of
which could wield a lightsaber.
He also used a deadly blaster
and a powerful energy staff,
which delivered fatal electric
shocks to his opponents.

Final battle
Grievous was
no match for
the combined
power of the
Jedi Obi-Wan
Kenobi and
Anakin
Skywalker.

Clone Soldiers

Although Sidious had started a war in the galaxy, he didn't want either side to win it. He wanted the war to go on just long enough for him to bring the Sith to power. He made sure that the Republic had an army of its own, so that each side was evenly matched. The Republic army consisted of well-trained clone soldiers and a variety of battle tanks, plus cannons, gunships, and space assault ships.

For many battles, the clone soldiers fought on the side of the Republic. The Jedi generals did not know that the clone soldiers were programmed to be loyal to Sidious. When Sidious gave a special signal, the clone soldiers turned on their Republic masters, showing no mercy.

Weapons
Clone troopers carried powerful blasters and rifles.

Stormtroopers

When the war was over, Darth Sidious ruled the galaxy as Emperor Palpatine, and the clone soldiers became his personal army. He renamed them Stormtroopers and forced many millions of human males to join their ranks. Military Academies were formed in which new recruits were trained to be foot soldiers or more specialized troops, such as pilots or scouts. The Stormtroopers were trained to be totally loyal to the Empire.

Armor
Stormtrooper armor protected the soldier inside from weapon and bomb blasts.

Stormtrooper

122

The Stormtroopers could not be bribed or persuaded into betraying the Emperor. People everywhere learned to fear the sinister white-armored troops.

Snowtroopers
Some Stormtroopers wore specialized armor to protect them from the cold on freezing planets. They were called snowtroopers.

Vader's son
Luke was raised on Anakin's home planet, Tatooine, by his uncle and aunt.

Vader's daughter
Leia was raised on the planet Alderaan. She became a Princess—and a secret member of the Rebel Alliance.

Empire and Rebels

When Darth Sidious came to power, a dark age began in the galaxy—the Empire. As Emperor Palpatine, Sidious used his massive armies to terrify the galaxy and to stop anyone from rising against him.

Nevertheless, a secret opposition was formed, called the Rebel Alliance. The most famous Rebels were the children of Darth Vader, Luke and Leia.

When Anakin Skywalker turned to the dark side, he did not know that his wife, Padmé Amidala, was pregnant with twins. Tragically, Padmé died while giving birth. The twins were hidden away in separate places, so that Anakin would not find out about them.

Rebel Alliance
Leia and the Rebel Alliance plan an attack on the Empire from their secret base on the planet Yavin 4.

Han Solo
The Rebels welcomed any support they could get, even from former smugglers like Han Solo and Chewbacca.

Warrior upbringing
Jango was an orphan. He was raised by a legendary warrior army, thought to be the most dangerous in the galaxy.

Equipment
Jango wore a protective helmet to hide his identity. A jetpack allowed him to blast into the air and escape.

Jango Fett

The first clone troopers were cloned from a single "supreme warrior." He was a man named Jango Fett. Jango made his living as a bounty hunter. This means that he was paid to hunt criminals and outlaws. Darth Tyranus knew of his unbeatable combat skills and recruited him for the secret clone-army project.

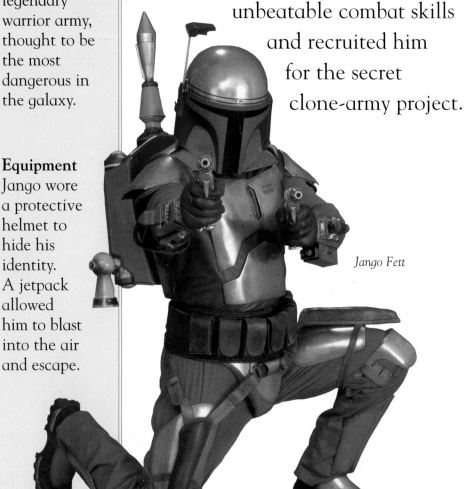

Jango Fett

Jango also carried out certain special missions for the Sith Lords. For example, he would assassinate any public figures that stood between the Sith Lords and their ultimate goal of ruling the galaxy. One such person was the good Senator Padmé Amidala. Thankfully, Padmé survived the attempts on her life, and the Jedi pursued Jango. Eventually, Jango was killed in a large battle between the Republic army and the droid army.

Jetpack
Jango uses his jetpack to attack Jedi Obi-Wan from above.

Flame thrower
Jango fires his deadly wrist-mounted flame thrower.

Zam Wesell

Airspeeder
When Zam needed to make a fast getaway, she jumped into her fast, green airspeeder.

Jango Fett had many contacts in the criminal underworld. One such contact was the hired assassin Zam Wesell. Zam was an alien whose species could shape-shift, which meant that she could change her body shape to imitate other species. This was useful when she needed to blend in with another planet's species without being noticed.

Jango hired Zam to carry out the daring murder of the politician Senator Padmé Amidala. First Zam tried to blow up the Senator's spaceship. Then, Zam released deadly insects called kouhuns into Padmé's bedroom while she slept, but her Jedi bodyguards were able to stop the attack in time. Zam was chased by the Jedi Obi-Wan Kenobi and Anakin Skywalker. They managed to capture her, but before she could give anything away, she was shot by a mysterious figure in the shadows—Jango Fett.

Jedi protector
Obi-Wan was trying to protect Senator Amidala.

True face
When shape-shifters die, they return to their own body shape.

129

Boba Fett

When Jango Fett was killed in battle, he left a young son named Boba. Young Boba had spent his whole life learning from his father, so when he grew up, he too became a bounty hunter. Boba inherited his father's armor and weapons, and became the best bounty hunter in the galaxy.

Boba often worked for Darth Vader, tracking down enemies of the Empire.

When Darth Vader learned that he had a son, he wanted to track him down and see if he could turn him to the dark side. He would have liked to rule the galaxy alongside his son.

Like father, like son
Boba Fett is an exact, unaltered clone of his father, Jango.

Secret weapons
Boba's armor conceals a deadly flame thrower and powerful rocket dart launchers.

Vader employed Boba Fett to find and capture Luke, but Luke was firmly on the side of good. He had begun to train as a Jedi and refused to turn to the dark side.

Boba was eventually defeated during a battle with Luke Skywalker and his allies. Boba Fett's jetpack was damaged, causing it to malfunction. It sent the bounty hunter soaring into the air, out of control. Fett finally tumbled to his death into the ravenous jaws of a giant desert creature called the Sarlacc.

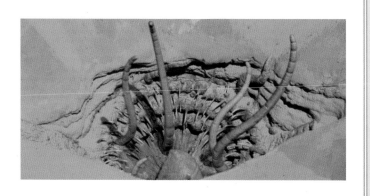

Armed spaceship
Boba traveled in his father's ship, "Slave I."
The ship was full of weapons.

Possible escape
Some people believe that Boba managed to escape from the stomach of the Sarlacc.

Jabba the Hutt

Another of Boba Fett's employers was a crime lord named Jabba the Hutt. This repellent slug-like creature was the leader of a large crime empire responsible for all kinds of shady deals, including murder, theft, and fraud.

Jabba lived in a palace on the desert planet Tatooine. He shared his palace with assorted gangsters, assassins, smugglers, corrupt officials, low-life entertainers, and servants.

Jabba paid Boba Fett to bring him a smuggler who owed him money. That smuggler was Han Solo, who had become friends with Luke and Leia Skywalker. When Han was captured and brought to Jabba, Leia set out with Chewbacca to rescue Han. When she was also captured, it was up to Luke to rescue all his friends. During Luke's rescue mission, Leia was able to wrap a chain around Jabba's neck and defeat him.

Bib Fortuna
Bib Fortuna ran Jabba's palace for him. He had a large head tail, sharp teeth, and scary red eyes.

Pet monster
Jabba kept a ferocious rancor monster in a cellar pit. Sometimes he fed it human captives for fun.

133

Rogues and Villains

Informer
Garindan was a low-life informer who lived on Tatooine.

Watto
Watto made Anakin and Shmi work very hard.

Even before the Empire took control, parts of the galaxy were wild and lawless. On remote planets like Tatooine, highly dangerous Podraces were organized, although they were officially banned. Slavery was also common. When the Jedi Qui-Gon visited Tatooine, he met a slave dealer named Watto. Watto owned Anakin Skywalker and his mother, Shmi. Anakin and Shmi both worked for Watto in his junk shop.

Under the Empire, crime was often rewarded. The Empire relied on spies to report suspicious behavior. Often, it forced officials to do its shady business.

When Darth Vader wanted to capture Luke Skywalker, he threatened to shut down an entire city if its leader, Lando Calrissian, did not lure Luke into a trap. When Vader broke his promise, Lando helped Luke and joined the Rebels.

Calrissian
Lando Calrissian had great charm.

Greedo
Greedo was a small-time hitman hired to kill Han Solo.

Imperial Might

The Empire kept control of the galaxy with its gigantic army of Stormtroopers and a fleet of warships

Heavy weapons
Star Destroyers were armed with many powerful weapons.

that patrolled all the major space routes. The biggest warship was Darth Vader's personal ship, the "Executor." The "Executor" led a fleet of Star Destroyers.

Each Star Destroyer had enough firepower to destroy entire planets. Swarming around these big ships were countless smaller TIE-fighters, each piloted by a fighter pilot.

When the Empire discovered a Rebel secret base on the ice planet Hoth, it sent in massive walking tanks called AT-ATs. Pilots controlled the tanks from a cockpit in the head. Until the battle of Hoth, AT-ATs were thought to be unbeatable in battle, but the Rebels toppled them by wrapping cables around their legs.

Scout walkers
Smaller AT-ST, or scout walkers, patrolled many planets.

Sinister spy
A probe droid spotted the Rebel base on Hoth and informed the Empire.

Torture
Onboard the
Death Star,
Darth Vader
threatened to
use a torture
droid on
Princess Leia
to make her
reveal the
whereabouts of
the Rebel bases.

Death Star

The Death Star was the Emperor's
most terrifying superweapon. It was
the size of a small moon, but it was
actually one of the largest starships
ever built. Its gigantic superlaser
weapon could destroy entire planets.
To demonstrate its enormous power,
the Empire used it to
destroy the planet of
Alderaan. This was
the planet on which
Darth Vader's
daughter, Leia, had
lived most of her life.

Fatal flaw
The unguarded exhaust port was located at the end of a long channel on the surface of the Death Star.

Mastermind
One of the Emperor's leaders, Grand Moff Tarkin, was the mastermind behind the Death Star.

Yet even the Death Star had a flaw. If a skilled pilot could fire torpedoes into a small exhaust shaft on the Death Star's surface, a chain reaction of explosions would blow up the entire starship. The Rebel Alliance sent their best pilots to reach the target. Luke Skywalker trusted in the Force and fired. A direct hit! Luke had managed to destroy the Empire's most terrible weapon.

Rebel Victory

The brave Rebels refused to give up the fight against Emperor Palpatine and his Empire of evil. Although the Emperor commanded the biggest army in the galaxy, he was not invincible. The Rebels teamed up with a band of forest-dwelling creatures called Ewoks on the planet Endor. Together they overpowered the Emperor's Stormtroopers and helped the Rebels' spaceships to launch an attack on the second Death Star.

Second Death Star
After the Rebels destroyed the first Death Star, Emperor Palpatine ordered that a replacement be built.

Look out!
The Ewoks only used weapons made of wood, yet they managed to defeat the well-trained and well-armed Stormtroopers.

Meanwhile onboard the Death Star, Luke battled for his life against the Emperor and Darth Vader. When Luke refused to turn to the dark side, the Emperor forced the father and son to fight. In the end, Luke could not kill Vader and when the Emperor tried to kill Luke, Vader turned against his Sith Master and threw him to his doom down a deep shaft.

Luke had proven that even those who have turned to the dark side still have good inside them that can be reached—if you only know how.

Vader unmasked
Luke lifted Vader's mask to gaze at the face of the father he had never known.

Glossary

Apprentice
A person who is learning a skill.

Assassinate
To kill a ruler or politician

Asteroid
A rock that floats in space.

Blaster
A gun that fires a deadly beam of light.

Bounty hunter
A person who hunts criminals and other wanted people, in return for money.

Clone Wars
The conflict between the Republic and the Separatists, who want to destroy the Republic.

Cyborg
Someone who is part-living matter and part-robot.

Dark side
The part of the Force associated with fear and hatred.

Death Star
A moon-sized superweapon developed by the Empire.

Droid
A kind of robot.

Emperor
The leader of an Empire is called an Emperor. Palpatine is the Emperor who rules the Galactic Empire.

Empire
A group of nations ruled by one leader.

The Force
An energy field created by all living things.

Force lightning
One of the Sith's powers that involved firing deadly electricity from their fingers.

Galaxy
A group of millions of stars and planets.

Jedi Knight
A *Star Wars* warrior with special powers who defends the good of the galaxy.

Jedi Council
The governing body of the Jedi order. The wisest Jedi, such as Yoda, sit on the Council.

Jedi Master
The most experienced Jedi of all.

Jedi Order
The name of a group that defends peace and justice in the galaxy.

Jedi Temple
The Jedi headquarters where the Jedi Council meets and Jedi live, train, and work.

Light side
The part of the Force associated with goodness, compassion, and healing.

Lightsaber
A Jedi's or Sith's weapon, made of glowing energy.

Lightspeed
A special kind of travel that allows a spaceship to cross vast distances of space in an instant.

Padawan
A trainee Jedi who is being instructed by a Jedi Master.

Parry
To ward off a strike from a lightsaber or other sword-like weapon.

Particles
Tiny pieces of something.

Rancor
A large and deadly reptile-like creature.

Reactor
A device in spaceships used to generate power for travel.

Rebel Alliance
A group of people who want to remove the Emperor from power.

Republic
A nation or group of nations in which the people vote for their leaders.

Senate
The governing body of the Republic.

Shield
An invisible protective barrier around a spaceship, planet, or other object.

Sith
Enemies of the Jedi who use the dark side of the Force.

Skiff
A small boat-like airspeeder.

Stormtroopers
Soldiers, many of them clones, who are loyal to Emperor Palpatine. They wear white armor.

Trade Federation
A group of merchants and transporters who control the movement of goods in the galaxy.

Wield
To handle a weapon or tool with ease.

Index

Index